Eyes with No Soul

Sheri Chapman

This book is a work of fiction. Names, characters, places and incidents are products of the author's imagination and are not to be construed as real. Any resemblance to actual events, locales, organizations, or persons living or dead, is entirely coincidental.

COPYRIGHT

Trient Press
3375 S Rainbow Blvd
#81710, SMB 13135
Las Vegas,NV 89180
www.trientpress.com

Ordering Information:
Quantity sales. Special discounts are available on quantity purchases by corporations, associations, and others. For details, contact the publisher at the address above.
Orders by U.S. trade bookstores and wholesalers. Please contact Trient Press: Tel: (775) 996-3844; or visit www.trientpress.com.

Printed in the United States of America

Publisher's Cataloging-in-Publication data
Chapman, Sheri
A title of a book :Eyes with No Soul
ISBN Paperback: 9781-953975-00-3
        E-book: 9781-953975-01-0

Thank you to Jean Anderson, my mom, and Norma Snyder, my aunt, for their feedback and encouragement on my first publication.

Chapter One

They say the eyes are a window to the soul. I've always found that to be true. *Especially now...*

I've always been inclined to experience extrasensory sensations; some might even call them premonitions. I, however, would just call them strong feelings. At times, I have the ability to read individuals I know especially well by understanding minute differences in their body language, but I *never* noticed it being more than that.

In one instantaneous moment, I graduated from awareness of minor sensations to the floodgates of perception being thrown wildly open, and I didn't like it. It put my life in danger.

I'd just been shopping with my friends at the food court in the mall when I accidentally bumped into a man. I turned toward him to excuse myself, and I found myself drowning in the blue icy depths of his rock-hard eyes. His cold mouth turned down into an unhappy frown when he saw my shocked reaction to his gaze. His eyes studied me intently then narrowed, almost as if he recognized me from somewhere.

In that moment, I drank in his rugged appearance. He reminded me of a clean construction worker. A hint of cologne floated about him as he stood directly before me. He was dressed in a tan and brown plaid shirt unbuttoned to the top of his chest, and a pair of well-worn jeans clasped his thighs. His feet were covered in fawn colored work boots.

He was of average height for a man, six feet or so by my guess, and lean but muscular with unkempt sandy hair. His square jaw sported a tired shadow of a beard. All in all, he was not an unattractive figure, but it was his eyes that swallowed up my attention and left me shaking.

In that very long moment, I knew what he had done; and he knew that I knew. I'd just bumped into my very first murder mystery. The only difference was that I had solved the crime; I just had no idea of who the victim was.

My heart was sledgehammer, pounding a rhythm on the jail bars in my chest. It was as if time had frozen when our eyes met. It took a nudge in the ribs from Angela to snap me back to the present. I quickly ripped my gaze from his, studied the floor tile, and muttered an apology to him before moving my concrete-filled legs into action – in the opposite direction – with as fast of a walk as they would go.

"Whoa, girlfriend," his deeply amused voice carried after me. "What are you running from?"

As if he didn't know.

I heard heavy steps bound after me. It was all I could do not to scream and run like a panicked rabbit. My four friends were walking quickly beside me, but they had no idea why I was acting so strangely. It took no premonition for me to understand this, for I was being shot many looks of puzzlement.

Strong fingers circled my upper arm, and I found myself being swirled around to face the very thing that would consume my future nightmares.

"What's the hurry, princess? Didn't you just bump into me?" His icy eyes imprisoned me and nearly stole my breath.

"Um, y-yes, I did, sir. I'm so sorry. I truly didn't mean to…" my voice trailed off.

"What's this 'sir' nonsense? Call me Adam. Come, sit." "Uh, I can't. My parents are expecting me." My eyes flashed at my friends, so they all jiggled their heads like bunch of nodding dolls.

"Oh, a few moments of your time won't hurt. I'll buy you and all of your little friends some Taco Bell."

"I- I really can't. Maybe some other time?" I felt locked in time, and I was desperate to escape.

His mouth reformed the granite-hard line, and chiseled words fell from his lips and shattered at my feet, "You can certainly count on that. Okay. I *will* see you around." His hand dropped from my arm and like a flash, he disappeared without a trace.

"What in the heck was all that about?" demanded Janice.

"I- I- I don't want to talk about it here. Can we please just go?" I managed to whisper.

"Sure, sweetie," Angela crooned. "We can talk about it in the car."

We piled in Kim's SUV. I sat shotgun. I'd hoped it would discourage the questions long enough for me to process what'd really happened, but it didn't stop me from feeling the three sets of eyes shooting inquisitive lasers in the back of my head.

"Okay, spill!" Janice stated firmly.

"Just… give me a moment," I said breathlessly.

"Sure, babe. Take all the ten minutes you need," Julie joked.

I shivered in the heat. School was almost out, and the weather was already unseasonably warm. Kim blasted the air, oblivious to my discomfort. I blinked my eyes, trying to stall the scene that yet again commanded my inner vision.

Blood. Blood spilled everywhere. On the walls, on the floor… I was sickened by the overpowering smell flooding my senses. I didn't see a body, just the thickening black pools and splatters staining the entire living room…

I bent forward to try to hide my reaction, a gag reflex. I took a steadying breath and turned to face my friends.

Worry was etched in their foreheads and eyes. Concern for my out-of-character actions overcame any playful antics.

"Laurie, are you alright?" Kim asked. Her focus on me was unwavering.

"No, not really," I said with a gulp. "Okay, you know how I always tease you guys and tell you I'm psychic?"

"You really get me going with that," said Kim. "You always know what's wrong with me without me even saying!"

"Yes, well, uh, I'm just really good at reading body language. I *know* you guys." I said. "But this is the first time that I've had a truly psychic episode…"

I took a moment to let that sink in. Comprehension widened their eyes.

"What happened?" Angela breathed. "What did you see?"

I shuddered, and goose bumps puckered my skin. "Blood. That's all I could see at first. It was so strong. It was all I could see... or smell."

Traces of doubt were reflected in Julie's eyes, but I think the others believed me.

I suddenly exclaimed, "That man is the devil. He killed someone, and he got away with it!"

"What are you going to do?" Angela asked.

"Oh, I don't know," I wailed. "They'd put me in a padded room with a nice tight white jacket if I go to the police and tell them I'm the next Allison DuBois."

"She has a point," Julie noted.

"So what, then?" asked Kim. "I noticed that you definitely perked his interest."

I shivered again. "That scared the crap out of me, too," I stated. "I think he knows I know… somehow."

"What if he's watching us to see what we're driving?" observed a wide-eyed Kim.

"Let's get out of here!" I said with the intensity I felt. The drive home was an apprehensive, quiet drive. Each was wrapped in her own thoughts. We paranoid ones would spy at the cars trailing behind. After pulling up to Kim's house, we quickly went in.

"You girls are home early," Kim's mother said as we came in.

"Ya, Mom. Can they stay for a while?"

"You know I love your friends," came the reply.

"Cool!"

We headed down to the naturally cool basement and theater room. It was really just a second living area with a few couches splashed here and there. Directly in front of the huge theater screen was a nice fluffy cream-colored rug littered with bright body pillows.

I plopped down and waited for the television screen to light up. I about choked when I saw the breaking news story flash.

The platinum blonde reporter began with a serious look on her painted face, "Darlene Houston has disappeared from her home in North Springfield early yesterday morning. The sixteen-year-old sophomore's parents were working the late shift and came home to a house splattered in blood. If you happened to know anything about Darlene and her disappearance, please contact the Springfield Police Department as soon as possible."

A picture of Darlene was plastered to the screen for the audience's perusal. Darlene was about 5'7", slender but shapely, and had dark hair and hazel eyes. She looked like a runner.

"Oh, my gosh!" Angela squeaked. "She looks a *lot* like you, Laurie!"

I couldn't breathe. I don't think I'd ever seen someone who looked more like me in my life. She could've been my sister… and nearly, but not quite, a twin. No wonder *Adam* had taken an interest in me!

The television camera turned to angle the house. Yellow police tape was crisscrossed everywhere. The camera zoomed in through the open door, and the picture that flashed on screen was an exact replica of the one in my head at the mall.

I took in a deep, sharp breath and went white as a sheet. My friends looked at me, then the screen. It dawned on them that *that* was the scene I'd been seeing for much of the afternoon.

"Oh, my God! Oh, my God! Oh, MY GOD!!!!" The girls were pacing and zipping around the room like hummingbirds after a feeder on a hot summer day. I just watched them in stunned silence.

"Laurie, we've got to do something! The police have to listen to you! We can all vouch some weird dude asked to buy us Taco Bell in the mall. We can say we saw blood on him and that he was interested in you. That should pique the police's interest! Your resemblance to that girl is uncanny!" Julie stated breathlessly.

"I guess…" I began. "I don't think I can lie and say I saw blood *on* him although I certainly did see blood when I looked at him!"

My friends nodded vigorously when they looked at me. "Do you think we should say something tonight?" I asked. "Or I could just talk to the school's resource officer tomorrow?"

"I think sooner is better than later, Laurie," said Kim. "Yes, but sweetie, if you're too scared or upset this evening, I don't think he'll kill anyone else tonight," Angela consoled.

"Hum. I just don't know what to do. I'm leaning toward waiting. At least I kind of know our SRO," I said picturing the police officer in my mind.

"Okay. It's decided then," said Julie. "Let's watch a movie to help get our minds off of it."

"Something funny?" I asked. "I really would like something light and airy. Maybe even an *Avengers* movie? They have corny humor that makes me laugh every time."

"Yeah, we know why you like the *Avengers* movies," Kim teased.

"Really?" I asked.

"Um, don't act like you don't know! Does Chris Hemsworth or Chris Evans ring a bell?" Julie asked sweetly.

"Whatever," I mumbled with pinked cheeks.

We were absorbed by the movie for a snatch of time. When it was finished, we all went home with anticipation about the big day in store for tomorrow.

I knew I wouldn't sleep well with all the bloody memories dancing in my head. I half way considered taking some medicine to help me sleep but decided against it. I tried to lie down, but each time I shut my eyes, red splashes spilled down the back of my lids.

Morning came before I was ready. She slapped me awake with a sharpness I didn't know she possessed. I sighed and got up. It was early, but I knew trying to go back to sleep was useless.

I slowly got ready and thought about what I was going to say to the police. How in the world would I explain all of this? How would I explain why I didn't call the police last night? Really, I had no proof; all I technically had was a gut feeling, and law enforcement would see that as a mere hallucination by the mind of an overactive, dramatic high school girl. They wouldn't give relevance to the fact that this guy seemed to possess stalking mannerisms and had indicated anger toward me, a girl who looked almost identical to his first victim. It was extremely disconcerting and spooky.

"Laurie, do you want me to fix you breakfast?" my mom called to me.

"No, it's okay, Mom. I don't have much of an appetite right now," I revealed.

Mom came into the bathroom where I'd just finished dabbing on a bit of perfume.

"Honey, I'm really worried."

"Me, too, Mom."

"You know why?" she asked.

"Well, I figure."

"I guess I should know that by now, huh?" she asked, affectionately rubbing my shoulder. "That girl looks like you," she observed.

"Yes, Mom, how can that be? Did I have a twin that you gave up for adoption or something? It's crazy how much that girl looks like me!"

"I agree, honey, but you know they say we all have a twin, a doppelganger, in this world."

"Okay… and mine got taken out. Nice."

"Oh, Laurie, they'll catch that man, don't worry!"

"Mom–"

"Yes?"

"I have something to tell you… I sort of… bumped into the killer yesterday."

"WHAT?"

"Well, Julie, Kim, Angela, Janice, and I all went to the mall to goof off, and I literally bumped into him."

"So why isn't he apprehended, then?" Mom asked, an incredulous look on her face.

"Mom, no one knows who killed that girl; only *I* do. They don't have a body; so technically, they can't say she was murdered."

"Okay, honey, so then how do you know this guy was the one?" She placed a hand on her hip but the concerned look on her face didn't diminish.

"Mom," I paused. "I know."

Mom saw the seriousness on my face. She must've considered that my entire life had been punctuated with correct premonitions.

"Oh, my God, baby! I've got to hire you a guard! You're right! You look too much like that girl! You're in danger! *Oh nooo!* What are we going to do?" Her hands were fluttering like the laundry on the line in the wind.

"MOM! Calm down. I'm going to talk to the school's police officer today and tell him what I know." I put my hands on her arms to help calm her.

"So this guy *saw* you, right?"

"Uh… yeah, Mom. He did." I dropped my unexpectedly leaden arms.

Suddenly, I was clutched in her arms so tightly I felt like there wouldn't be anything left when she finally let go. I returned her hug, not sure how this was all going to work out.

"Mom, I've got to go now. I promise to be careful. I want to get to school early so I can talk to Officer Heitz."

"Oh, alright, darling. But *be careful*!!! Send me a text when you get to school."

"Will do, Mom. Have a good day."

"You, too, honey. I'll see you tonight. If you need me, call. I'll be there. Don't go back to the mall or be alone. I love my baby so much!"

"Okay. I promise to stay with friends in Ozark, I promise to call you, and I love you, too. More."

"Nope."

"Yup. 'Bye, now!"

After Mom left, I packed my stuff into my black Escalade truck and headed to school. When I pulled up and parked, I had to gather the courage to go in. I felt like I'd be a spectacle for the world to see. Not everyone would know I bumped into the murderer and was now on his radar, but they'd see my similarities to the victim. That alone would make me an object of attention. You know how high school is: *anything for gossip.*

Sheri Chapman

15

Chapter Two

I went directly to Officer Heitz's office. He must've been off patrolling some unloading zone for one of our schools. That was okay. I'd just wait for him... And try to breathe.

Just then, my phone buzzed with a text from Julie. *"Hey, girl. I saw ur truck in the lot. Where ya at?"*

"In Officer Heitz's office."

"Okay. I'll be right there."

I felt consoled to not be in this alone. Support was always welcomed!

Julie and I didn't have to wait long for Officer Heitz to show. He issued us into his office. He sat in his chair behind his desk and waited for us to begin.

Officer Heitz was a fit, fairly tall blonde man in his early thirties. He had inquisitive blue-green eyes. Something about his demeanor was comforting.

"How can I help you today?" he inquired solicitously. "Oh, boy... how do I begin?" I asked. My face must have reflected my frustration because I could see understanding register in his eyes followed by a softening of his features.

"Are you having difficulty with another student?" he prompted.

"No, she's having trouble with a murderer," Julie interjected.

Immediately, the officer's relaxed aura switched to alert. I knew that not only was Officer Heitz a school resource officer, but also that he worked for the police department when school wasn't in session. It was a small comfort.

"What's this?" he asked.

"Yesterday, my friends and I went to the mall," I began. "I accidentally bumped into this man. He really scared me."

Officer Heitz appeared to relax a bit. I was sure he probably thought I was a silly little high school girl with an over-active imagination after hearing about the only brutal murder in the history of our demographics.

"What did he do that scared you?" he asked.

"He stalked her. He acted really weird around her," Julie began. "I mean, *look at her,* Officer Heitz! She looks exactly like the victim!"

Officer Heitz did appear to study me more closely, and his eyes widened just a bit.

"Look, ladies. I'm sure you were scared, but unless this guy did something like threaten you, I'm afraid there isn't anything I can do. Do you know this guy's name?"

"Adam. At least that is what he told us."

"Do you have a last name? Can you describe him? I feel it is worth checking out, especially because Ms. Bowman's appearance *is* so very similar to the victim's," he tried to console.

We described the man to the best of our abilities. I could recall every last detail. The SRO took notes until we'd finished.

"I have just a few more questions," Officer Heitz began. "What age range is he in? Did you see what he was driving?"

"No, he disappeared after promising to see Laurie again," Julie said.

"And he looked late twenties to me," I added.

"And you've never seen this guy before?" clarified the officer of the law.

"Never," we both admitted.

"Okay. I'll see what I can do. Just know that my hands are tied as far as the law is concerned. I'd give you a strong bit of advice, however, Ms. Bowman. You *do* resemble the victim. Quite a bit, actually. Don't go anywhere alone. Use the buddy system. I see you running a lot. Don't run alone. Keep jogging with your two buddies I always see you with. Let everyone know where you are at all times."

"Yes, sir. And thank you." I shook his hand before I left his office.

I walked straight to the library with Julie trailing in my wake. I went straight to the couch studying the newspaper and magazine racks and sunk wearily onto its soft hardness.

"Are you okay?" asked Julie.

"Not really. Officer Heitz is right. I mean, nothing's really happened," I wailed as quietly as I could. "What can be done until he attacks me? Maybe I won't ever see him again; I hope I don't!"

"Laurie, you did everything you could. You gave the police a description of the guy. You can't prove he did it, but at least your resemblance to that poor girls helps with your credibility. Be consoled and take Officer Heitz's advice. Be very cautious and go nowhere alone. Okay?"

"Okay," I sighed wearily and got up. "Mom does know what's going on. I talked to her this morning. I guess we need to head to class. Come on. We can get a pass. We should be excused because we were talking to the security officer."

The day passed by at a surprising regular pace. The times where I was busy and engaged went quickly, where the times when I had to work independently and had time to think went by very slowly.

Why should I be so worried? I mean, he doesn't even know my name! The chances he saw what we drove were minimal. I really had nothing to fear, did I? Still, I would take precautions. *It was my life I was talking about.*

In the halls, I met a few strange or curious looks, but as a whole, I was relatively left alone as far as gossip went. I needed to give credit where credit was due.

After school I met up with Julie and Kim.

"Are we running today?" Kim asked.

"I need to. Nothing is better for stress relief. Are you guys in?" I asked.

"Definitely!" my friends responded in unison.

We dressed out and put our things in our cars. We took off to run our typical five miles. The trees swayed seductively over the edges of the sparkling Finley River waters as we jogged by. A bird sang a melody to the rhythm made by our feet, and an angry squirrel scolded us for interrupting the peace. All couldn't be so bad in the world. *Could it?*

"So what happened today?" asked Kim.

Julie and I filled her in. We also told her what Officer Heitz suggested and how I would use the buddy and texting system to let others know where I was at all times.

"Not to be the devil's advocate," I began, "but you know you guys were all there with me, too. He could target you as well. Kim, I'm not trying to scare you, but *if* he tried to see what we were driving, we were in *your* car. I want you to be as careful as I'm going to be."

Kim had the decency to go pale. She nodded her head in comprehension. This was very serious stuff to all of us. I only hoped we were over reacting.

"I think we need to have a slumber party this whole weekend," I said. "I think it'll help us all to be together and think this thing through. We can prepare if we have to."

"I agree," Kim said. "My house is perfect. Mom won't care. Come crash with me!"

"Sounds like a plan," Julie piped in.

"Okay. When we end our run, I'll let Angela and Janice know."

After we finished, I texted our other friends about the details and went home to shower as well as gather the stuff I'd need for the weekend. We planned to stay in Ozark. We didn't want to risk going to Springfield again, even though passing time at the mall was a favored recreational thing to do. We decided to see Channing Tatum's latest movie at the B&B Theater in Ozark.

Before I headed over to Kim's house, I waited for Mom to come home from work. I wanted to make sure she knew my plans for the weekend and that it was okay with her. I also wanted to let her know what Officer Heitz had said.

For a surprise, I decided to cook a nice dinner while I waited for Mom. I knew I wouldn't see much of her since I planned on being with my friends, so some nice time together would be welcomed.

I began boiling water for spaghetti noodles while slicing up French bread to butter then season with garlic salt and sprinkle with cheese. I loved my bread toasted, so I turned on the oven to preheat. I tossed together a garden salad.

By the time Mom got home, everything was prepared and set neatly on the table. Her pleased surprise was evidenced on her face.

"Oh, baby! What a nice surprise! Thank you!"

I loved doing things for my Mom. She was the best parent anyone could ever hope for. I liked to show my appreciation for her.

She was a paralegal for an extremely nice lawyer. She had a great job, and I realized how hard it could be when you had to be a parent and the sole provider; I did what I could to help.

We always enjoyed sitting down to a nice family dinner. Mom filled two bowls with the salad and placed garlic bread topped with bubbling cheese on napkins while I spooned noodles onto our plates and topped it with the aromatic home cooked sauce. The onions, mushrooms, and tomatoes mixture was chunky yet somehow smooth. My stomach growled in anticipation.

While we ate, I explained my plans to my mom. She was on-board because she was helping her boss with an important case, and she had to work a lot over the weekend.

"I feel bad, baby," she said, "I shouldn't be leaving you alone in a time like this."

"Mom, I won't be alone. I'll be at Kim's with her parents, Julie, Angela, and Janice. I think we're going to the movies tonight in Ozark. I'll keep in contact with you. Promise."

"Thanks, hon. I couldn't ask for a better daughter."

"And I couldn't ask for a better mother."

She kissed me bye and left at the same time I did so that she could do more research for her case. I went directly to Kim's.

The drive there was pleasant. Ozark was a suburb of Springfield, yet it had a small-town feel. It wasn't too "citified" for my tastes. I found that the nature contained in her frame was a great distraction.

Ozark was nestled in hilly country where trees were abundant. Oaks of many varieties, maples, elms, walnuts, and more deciduous trees congregated amongst the pines and cedars. Flanking them were many varieties of flowering trees. The pink and purple blends of peach tree blossoms, red bud trees, pink dogwoods, and lilacs were serenaded by the whites of still more dogwoods, lilacs, and other varieties.

The vegetation gathered to whisper around the profusion of lakes, streams, and rivers. Water ways were already being invaded by kayaks and canoes. John boats were perched on lakes and ponds of all sizes. I smiled at the simple beauty of the natural landscape already tolerating the anxiousness of people wanting to be free from the claustrophobia of winter time jail.

"It's about time you got here," I was admonished as soon as I walked in the door.

"Sorry. I had to spend a little time with my mom. She's got a busy weekend planned – of work. I won't get to see her much for that reason and because I'm staying here with you all."

"Yes, that's true," Kim agreed.

"I say let's head out to the movie. The one we want to see starts at 9:30. Let's get there in time to get good seats and refreshments."

"Okay. I'm not hungry at all, but I've gotta have some popcorn saturated with butter!" I exclaimed.

We headed out to the movies, parked, and went in. The time with my friends was perfect. The popcorn was terrific, and the theater was amazing. Of course, we loved the movie. All too soon, it was time to go.

"Wait just a minute. I need to use the facilities," I revealed as soon as we left the theater room. My stomach suddenly was clutched in a vice. Fleetingly, I wondered if I'd consumed too much grease. I went to the ladies' room to splash water on my face.

Within a few minutes, I returned. My stomach pain had eased, but I still felt a bit off.

"Laurie, are you okay?" Janice asked. "You look pale all of a sudden."

"Um, I feel kind of funny. I've got a weird, tingly feeling. I don't like it."

"Do you need to sit down?"

"No, I think I'm okay."

We headed for the door, but the closer to the exit we got, the funnier I began to feel. Immediately, I felt like I was walking through invisible quick sand. Each step pulled and sucked at my feet as I tried to approach the exit. A wall of tiredness built itself up around me and a blanket of goose bumps wrapped me in its folds. That's when the premonition hit me.

"We're being watched."

My statement was met with no skeptical looks this time. We began to nervously glance around. There were people trickling out of the theater here and there, but it certainly wasn't crowded. The majority of movie goers were home at 11:30 at night. I didn't see anyone paying us any undue attention.

"Well, I've been wrong before," I said doubtfully, but I just couldn't shake the feeling.

"Let's go. There's safety in numbers," Julie said.

"I say let's cruise by the police station. If we're being followed, that would surely discourage them," Angela mentioned.

"That's a GREAT idea!" I agreed.

We quickly scurried into the parking lot and piled into Kim's SUV. No one had to tell Kim to hurry. She turned the engine to life and shot out of our parking spot like a dove released from a magician's sleeve. While we were in line to pull out onto the main road, I saw the lights flip on in a blacked out '69 Dodge Charger.

Dukes of Hazzard, look out, I thought.

The Charger squealed its tires when it pulled out of the lot, leaving a trail of rubber burned into the pavement as it hurried to catch us. It was merely seconds before it zoomed up behind us as we turned onto the main road.

"You know this nut?" I asked Kim.

"No, but I don't like the way he's tail-gaiting!" she said with aggravation.

"Uh, neither do I," I said gritting my teeth. "It's kinda scaring me."

He was really close, nearly on our bumper.

"Do you know anyone at school who drives that car?" asked Angela. "It's pretty noticeable if you ask me!"

"I agree. And no, I don't," Julie said, "but he's got a road rage problem! We didn't even do anything to piss him off."

"Oh, boy!" Angela exclaimed. "We've found who was watching us, haven't we?"

"How about that police station?" I reminded in a breathless tone.

Kim's SUV was picking up speed, but so was the black car. He zoomed on the left side of us, revving his engine for effect, and squealed his tires as he rushed into the on-coming passenger's lane.

"What is he doing?" yelled Kim.

"I don't know!" I answered. "I'm hoping he doesn't try to ram us!"

Kim swerved to the right just after the words left my lips. All of us stifled screams because precisely at that moment, the black car slammed into our SUV. If Kim hadn't anticipated his move, we'd have been tuna in a can. Kim's reflexes had allowed us to narrowly miss a pole. I believed that the driver's intention had been to crash us into the supporting column. In between moments of panic, it made me wonder vaguely if he'd been a Demolition Derby driver.

"Oh, God!"

"Try to be calm, Kim," Janice soothed. "We can't let him run us off the road. Who knows what he'd do to us? We can't tell whose driving or how many people are in the car with his windows blacked out like that."

"He's blocking our way to the police department," Kim said in a scared voice.

"If you can turn around, head out toward Branson. Cops always sit between Wal-Mart's exit and Highway EE. If we speed, we'll get a cop's attention. If there isn't a cop, we'll take the EE exit and drive to town the back way. If he's not from Ozark, he won't anticipate that move."

"Yes, that's a good thought," answered Janice, "but I don't like driving away from a higher concentration of people."

"I agree," said Julie.

Everyone was quiet, gripping her seat with white knuckles and saying prayers.

"Hey, I've got a great idea! None of us are using our brains because we're panicked. I'm calling 911!" Julie whipped out her phone and pushed the corresponding buttons.

Kim had managed to spin the SUV in the opposite direction and fishtailed onto the exit ramp. The jerk in the car was right on our tail. Our vehicle had the bigger mass, but his was faster. He showed us this by ramming into us a few times. Every time he hit us, we'd scream and pitch forward.

Most of the time the black devil was too close for me to get a license number for Kim's phone call. Finally, when we surged forward from the last impact, I saw a heavy, black, home-made protective bumper of sorts on the front of the Charger where a license should be. I realized that
was how he kept his car from getting damaged.

I could hear Julie speaking into the phone between panicked screams. She told the police our plan with a breathless yet excited voice. She paused to look at us and revealed they had an officer on the way. She told us to take the next exit.

We sped toward Wal-Mart where safety awaited. Speedy Gonzalez was hot on our tail.

Kim nearly screamed, "He's going to try to pass us again!"

"Well, don't let him! Drive in the middle," I instructed. "Your car is heavier and bigger. Don't let him by you!"

Kim's tires screeched as she plowed into the middle of the highway. We all saw the quickly approaching bridge over the Finley River. Silently each recalled the steep drop before one would reach the water's edge. It wouldn't be a pleasant journey; it was one that might take you into another world. None of us wanted to verbalize our fears. *Did the driver plan to crash us into the waters below?* Kim punched the accelerator further, encouraging her racing steed to give her all it had to give. The RPMs whined as it responded. Finally, our destination was a tenth of a mile away!

When we veered off the Wal-Mart exit, I saw a police vehicle's lights and heard the scream of the siren quickly approaching. I couldn't picture a more handsome knight in shining armor to slay the famous black dragon!

The Dodge continued racing down the highway and was swallowed up by the night. Because he hadn't followed us up the ramp, I assumed he must've had a scanner in that devil of a car.

Kim pulled over as soon as the policeman met us at the top of the ramp. She slammed her vehicle into park and jumped out on shaky legs. She had to grab the door to keep from collapsing due to the effects of the subsiding adrenaline.

"Officer, he must have gone on toward EE!" She breathlessly exclaimed.

The officer was on his radio in a flash. I could hear the response. I sure hoped they could get an officer to pull that guy over. I'd feel a whole lot safer.

"You girls need to come down to the station for a little bit. We need to fill out a report of this incident."

"Yes, sir. Do you mind if we just follow you? I really don't care to go off by myself again. We're pretty shook up."

"Yes, of course. Calm down first. Then I'll drive, and you can follow me there."

"Thank you, Officer."

"Certainly."

Kim texted her mother what had happened and that we'd be home in a bit.

"You know, your mom is probably already in bed." "I'm sure," Kim replied. "I just want her to know why we aren't home if she is awake, or if she happens to wake up."

"I'd do the same thing," I began, "but I'm not going to text my mom. I know she'd have a fit. Besides, we're safe now." I couldn't help a warning thought from popping into my head: *famous last words…*

After about fifteen minutes had passed, we felt substantially calmer. Kim was able to follow the officer down town to the police department.

"Please, each of you fill out a statement of what happened," instructed the helping official. "If you can remember anything about the car, the driver, or if you happened to get his license, write that down, too."

"Officer, I didn't see a license. He either didn't have one or only had one on the back," I stated.

The look on the policeman's face wasn't encouraging.

When we finished our written statement, the official collected them. Then he informally interviewed us as a group.

Luckily, Kim's SUV only suffered minor damage. There was a scrape down the front driver-side fender. A bit of back paint from the car outlined the silvery metal where indeed, the two vehicles had collided. The back bumper was slightly dented. That was a blessing after all the ramming that he'd done.

At long last, the police released us to go home. It was an apprehensive drive back to Kim's. We were quiet in the car and wore solemn faces. When we pulled up, we quickly went in. We headed straight for the basement and put on comfy night clothes.

"I guess you know that means we won't be sleeping tonight," I stated the obvious.

"Yes, that dose of adrenaline was much too large," Janice agreed.

We stayed up most of the night. I think it was about six a.m. before any of us fell asleep.

About five hours later, we woke to find Kim's mother waiting. We had to explain the whole story to her.

"Oh, boy!" she exclaimed with a fiercely protective look on her face. "This is just terrible!"

"Mom, I don't know what else we can do!" Kim said. "I mean, we've talked to the police twice in one day."

"How bad is the damage to your car? Thank God you all have some wits about you!"

"I think the front diver's fender will need repaired and painted, and the bumper is dented, but I can live with it. It's not that bad, considering."

Chapter Three

The rest of the weekend and the following few weeks were full of boredom and of us feeling like we were being punished. Our parents wouldn't let us out of their sight. It felt like we couldn't go anywhere or do anything of account.

Finally, after the passage of the third uneventful week, our parents agreed that we could go to a birthday party being thrown by one of our friends on a Friday night. It was a bon fire party that went on into the night. Of course, we weren't allowed to drive there; our parents insisted on dropping us off.

"Oh, I just don't think I can take much more of this," Janice stated. "I love our parents and all, but I just can't stand feeling like a caged bird!"

"Agreed," said Angela. "But I can't stand the feeling of trying to be killed while we're just innocently driving, either."

I sighed heavily. "Yes, I agree with that, too. At least we get to do something tonight."

"Uh, huh!" both Julie and Kim said in unison.

"Sylvia's house is super sweet," I said.

Sylvia had a huge game room for us to play Foos ball, pool, and air hockey. Her family also owned a nice in-ground pool. There was a massive yard that bordered wooded acres for us to play Frisbee or whatever in.

After arriving at the party, we were greeted by a lot of our friends. It seemed our whole sophomore class was present as well as many upperclassmen. After a few hours of activity, Sylvia's parents began an enormous cook out. They seemed to barbeque every kind of meat under the sun.

There was also coleslaw, potato salad, chips of every variety, breads galore, and cake. Punch, soda, and tea were served to accompany.

"Sylvia sure can throw a party!" Janice said.

"Oh, yeah, baby!" I agreed.

Surprisingly, most of our friends only minimally talked to us about the car incident. I was compared to the victim a lot when the news first televised the murder, but as time went by and the headlines mentioned her less, the amount of comparisons between the two of us diminished as well.

As the night progressed, I had the sneaking suspicion we were being watched again. This time, however, I didn't feel the simultaneous strangeness. It was more just a gentle nudge of awareness than anything; I wasn't freaked out in the least. I happened to mention it to Angela.

"What do you think the difference is?"

"Hum. I don't really know. Maybe it's because whoever is watching us isn't a threat? I really don't get the impression that it's the same person."

"Really? You can tell whether you're in danger or not by the way you feel?"

"Well, I guess that is a pretty good way to put it."

We both began to discreetly look around.

"I think I see the culprit," Angela observed.

"Really? Who is it?"

"It's that really tall guy over toward the meat table."

"Oh. I think I see who you're talking about."

"How could you not?" Angela laughed. "He's almost as tall as the house."

The guy Angela pointed out was fairly new to our district. When I say fairly new, I meant he'd transferred in two or three years ago. He'd been going to our high school most of his experience, but he wasn't a native to our area.
That was why I didn't really know him.

Jacob was an eighteen-year-old senior who played football and basketball. He was a shade under 6'6" and was lean and muscular. In my opinion, he was a tall drink of water!

Jacob had olive-green eyes and very dark hair. When our eyes met briefly, I saw them widen in surprise. Perhaps he thought he could watch me and not be caught. I tried to hide my amused grin by turning back to Angela.

"Well, I'm certainly relieved," she stated.

"I knew it wasn't a bad feeling," I explained. "It just feels *different*, somehow, when I'm in danger. There's like urgency, or an edge if you will, to the way I feel. Sorry. I didn't mean to scare you."

"I don't know if I was really scared. I mean, what could happen with a million people around?"

"Nothing," I began. Then I scolded her, "but don't ever ask that question."

Angela grinned at my silly superstition. "Okay. Will do."

"I think I'm hungry," I stated. Angela's laugh tinkled around me like millions of tiny bells.

"Go for it, girlfriend," she whispered with a wink.

I tentatively went over to the table stuffed with savory meats. I evaluated which delicate selections I wanted to try. I did my best to look absorbed in the choices rather than sidetracked by my interest in a tall handsome guy standing nearby. Suddenly, a huge man's arm reached toward me with a Styrofoam plate.

As I took the plate from him, I looked up into his towering height and was greeted by twinkling green eyes and a smile punctuated with deep dimples.

"Oh, um, thank you."

"You're welcome. I always like to give a helping hand," he stated while his smile deepened.

"Jacob, right?"

"That's what I prefer to be called," he answered. "And you're Laurie, correct?"

"Yes. Nice to formally meet you."

"Likewise."

"You played football, right?"

"Yes, I did. And basketball."

"I can see that."

"Is that a tall joke?"

I smiled but shook my head. I selected a small chicken breast grilled to perfection. Barbeque sauce clung on ways that should be illegal. Next, I selected some Taco flavored Doritos and a tad bit of potato salad. I poured a sweet tea, all with the comforting help of an attentive man.

"Do you mind if I join you?" he asked. I could sense his nervousness.

"No, not at all. In fact, I would enjoy it," I encouraged. We found an uninhabited bench and sat. We began to eat.

"So… you're fairly new to Ozark. Where did you move from?" I began.

"I actually grew up on a small farm just on the other side of Minnesota, in Wisconsin. It was quaint and peaceful."

"Really? What made you and your family move here?' "Oh, there were a few reasons. Dad wanted to move down here to be closer to his mom so he could help take care of her. Then Mom wanted to move down here for her job. But that didn't pan out."

"The job?"

"No. Mom. She really wanted to move down here to see her boyfriend."

"Oh. I'm sorry."

"Don't be. We weren't ever really all that close. She isn't a woman in touch with her emotions."

An awkward silence followed his statement. I ate some more and drank to fill in the void. He did likewise.

"So you grew up here?"

"Oh, pretty much. I moved a little bit while in elementary, but I've been here since the fourth grade."

"That's cool."

"Kind of the same story as yours, only my dad left us." "I see," he stated. "Hardly anyone stays married these days. Makes you wonder why we still even try."

"Everyone thinks their situation will be different. It's hard work, and people are lazy; both have to give 100% or more, not 50/50."

"That's true," he paused to give an appropriate break before a subject change. "So, do you play any sports?"

"Track and cross country. That's about it. I'm not that coordinated."

"You look pretty coordinated to me." He said it with a straight face, and his eyes stayed glued on mine. He deserved kudos for that.

"Um, thank you," I laughed. "Give it time. You'll come around to my way of thinking. You've never seen me throw a ball."

I saw his eyes light up.

"Oh, *n-n-no!*" I said adamantly.

"Oh, yes!" he answered.

He took my plate and threw both of our trash away before dragging me to the field. My eyes searched for a friend to rescue me, but not one could be seen. Darn them! I'd bet money they were watching!

The only kind of ball I was somewhat comfortable with, of course, was a soccer ball. I got to use my feet, not my hands. Hands on me were only meant to be used to achieve balance when I ran a fairly straight line.

Jacob picked up a football. Gently, he tossed it to me. Let me tell you, it wasn't pretty. I tried to catch the crazy thing, but like a wild animal escaping from a trap, it squirmed up through my fingers and bounced on the ground. I tried to seize it, but I'm sure I resembled someone trying to pick up a fish flopping on the ground. When I went left, it went right. Finally, I managed to grab it.

When I looked up, Jacob coughed into his hand. It sounded suspiciously like a laugh. I felt frustrated, but of course, I couldn't show it. Much.

"*See?*" I said. I could feel embarrassment flushing my cheeks.

"Throw it to me."

"So you can have some more fun at my expense?"

"No. I want to teach you."

"Why? I don't think I'll ever be on the team."

He smiled gently at me. I was a sucker for his dimples. I found myself smiling back. So, I raised my hand and gave it a whirl.

How he caught my terrible throw, I'll never know. I think footballs were supposed to spin, not go end over end. He came slowly toward me with the football.

He stood behind me, his body touching mine as he placed the football in my hand. He carefully arranged the strange object in my hand until I was holding it correctly. He tried to tell me how to release the ball when I threw it, but it was like trying to understand a foreign language. However, I did try.

He worked with me on catching and throwing about thirty minutes. I did improve, but I also think he knew
when to end a good thing.

We walked back toward the house, and because we were warm, the pool caught our attention.

"Want to swim?" he asked.

"Uh, I – um, want to see what my friends are doing first."

I noticed him slowing his step.

"You're welcome to join us," I said quickly.

"Oh. Sure," he said.

I saw my friends coming outside with drinks. They saw us, and we were ushered over.

"Do you all feel like swimming?" I asked.

"Give us a bit, and maybe," Janice replied.

"Cool," I said looking up at Jacob. He smiled down at me.

We pulled up a couple of chairs. I introduced Jacob to my friends, and we quickly were involved in many matters of interest.

"So, I guess you heard about that murder in Springfield," Jacob said when fresh topics appeared to dwindle. We all must have had quite a look on our faces, because Jacob said, "I'm sorry. Was she a friend of yours?"

"No," I said. "We're just really… interested in the case." Jacob looked straight at me and asked, "Are you related to her?"

I looked away and said, "No."

"Oh, wow."

"Yes, she looks quite a lot like her, huh?" Julie guessed his thoughts.

"Yes, she does!" he exclaimed.

I looked back at Jacob. "Have you heard of any new developments on the case?" I inquired.

"Not that the police are releasing," he replied.I couldn't help but look surprised.

"My dad's a bounty hunter," he revealed. "He goes into the station all the time. He has some good friends on the force."

"Oh, really? That's cool!" I said genuinely.

"It has its quirks," he replied. "It can be a dangerous way to make a living, and it's hot or cold as far as the money is concerned."

"So does he work with a bail bondsman?" I prompted.

"Much of the time, yes. Sometimes he just goes for reward money. Other times, banks hire him to repossess things. Bondsmen are his biggest employer although the banks run a close second."

"I suppose so."

"He likes the detective work almost as much as the adrenaline thrill," he added.

We nodded our heads with wide eyes.

About ten minutes later, Kim announced, "Well, I'm ready to swim."

We donned our swim wear and played in the water for an hour. Jacob dunked and threw us a few times. Then we'd play silly games like *Marco Polo*. It was a blast. Finally, it was time to head home.

Kim's dad picked up us. I waived bye to Jacob who watched us leave. Of course, I was the brunt of many snickers in the car ride home, helpful and not-so-helpful suggestions, and elbow nudges.

Once at Kim's, we headed down the stairs. We'd all crash on the second living room floor (the theater room) for the night. Surprisingly within an hour, we were all drifting off to sleep.

The black demon landed in the tree outside my window and just watched me. Its yellow eyes glowed in the dank night, and its slit red pupils pulsed with hunger. The scarlet color symbolized the blood of his victims, both past and present.

The shadow of death was a carrion bird waiting for the last throws of death before it landed to feed. It anticipated ripping into the soft body tissues almost as much as it enjoyed feasting on the flesh. A shiver of excitement shook it slightly and a nictitating membrane passed over the alien eyes.

It reached toward the window, the only barrier separating the two of us. Slowly, it extended a morbidly long talon, sharp and cruelly curved, and began to test the glass. I sat up to better see.

It reacted by curling back paper-thin lips to reveal huge yellow and black stained canines that sliced and snapped at the wet night air. Foul breath snaked up in a hot column as it hissed frustration at its discovery. A five-foot snake tongue immerged and licked the window. It suctioned itself to a piece of glass.

A tiny etching noise began as I noticed its claw beginning to trace a rough circle on the glass. It was going to enter by removing a section of glass…

I sat up with a sharp intake of breath. The feeling of danger nearly overpowered me as premonition set in. The dream wasn't a dream at all! A figure dressed in black could barely be distinguished against the back drop of the night sky. A tool was in his hand, and he was tracing a rough circle in a section of glass!

I screamed and yelled for everyone to get up. We took off toward the stairs and barreled up them as fast as humanly possible. We must've sounded like a herd of wild elephants screaming like banshees as we approached Kim's parent's room.

Kim's father materialized before us. I screamed at him to get a gun. He reappeared quickly with a .45 caliber pistol in his hand.

"He's in the basement!" I screamed.

"Mom, call the police!" Kim yelled with a panicked voice.

The house was in complete chaos for fifteen minutes. Of course, the culprit had disappeared when he realized he no longer had stealth on his side. Kim's parents ran outside to check the perimeter.

"Don't disturb any possible evidence," I gently reminded from the doorway.

"You've watched too many *Dateline* murder shows," Julie managed to tease. "I doubt they'll even collect evidence since no major crime occurred."

"He intended to commit a major crime."

"True, but you know how the law is. You can't be convicted on your intentions, only on your actions."

I sighed wearily. I knew that was true. Breaking and entering was a felony, but it wasn't nearly as heinous as kidnapping with intent to murder!

The police were out in ten minutes. Another night's sleep went by the way side. There were questions to be answered, details to collect, and a lot of time was spent with whatever else police do. It was probably 5:00 a.m. before the law left Kim's.

I was exhausted, but I certainly didn't feel like sleeping. I overheard Kim's parents talking about installing an alarm. Who could blame them?

Sheri Chapman

Chapter Four

Several hours later, I was home in my own bed. I was so tired, but I knew I wouldn't be able to sleep. Mom had given me some medicine to help relax me, and sleep finally overtook my mentally fatigued body.

I woke up hours later. I felt rested at last. Mom must've heard me up and about, because she had started frying sausage for a biscuit gravy meal. I came down stairs and opened up the biscuit can and spread the dough sections out on a pizza pan. She'd just started adding the milk to the future gravy, so I popped the bread in the oven.

"I've made a decision, babe. I'm going to hire a detective. *I want that guy apprehended.*"

"But Mom – that might be expensive."

"I'm sure. But money doesn't matter if there's anything I can do to protect you or possibly save your life."

"Oh, Mom. I love you!" I wrapped my arms around her waist and rested my head on her shoulder. She returned the embrace. I pulled back and said, "If I can't talk you out of this–"

She shook her head.

"Well, this guy I go to school with… actually, his *dad* is a bounty hunter. They do detective work in their profession. I bet he would do it. He might not be nearly as expensive. It might be worth checking out."

"Oh, there's this *guy*, huh?"

Mom's teasing smile made me happy. She'd been way too sober and anxious up until this point. I felt my cheeks growing warm. She lifted my chin so I looked her in the eyes.

"Who's this… *guy*?"

"Hahaha! I told you, I go to school with him. He's a big football and basketball player."

"Oh, he's really into it?"

"Yes, and literally, he's *BIG*." I giggled again. "He's almost 6"6.

"Oh, my! That *is* big."

"Yes, it is. I think I'll text him and ask him if his dad might be interested. Is that okay?"

"Sure, baby. I just have to do something!" The seriousness was back.

"Okay, Mom. I'll text him right after we eat."

The gravy was thickening and bubbly under Mom's constant stirring, and the aroma was making my taste buds water. I opened up the oven door and found the biscuit tops were lightly golden brown and done to perfection. I donned an oven mitt and retrieved the bread.

It was self-serve banquet style. We filled our plates with piping hot food, filled our cups with ice-cold orange juice, and sat down.

"Thanks, Mom."

"For what, baby? Being a mom?"

"Yup. Isn't it nice to have appreciation?"

"You know it!"

After eating, we cleaned the kitchen. Then I went to my room to text Jacob and do some homework.

"Hey, Jacob. This is Laurie."

"Hey. I was beginning to wonder if I'd hear from u."

"Really?"

"Ya".

"Well, I didn't hear from u?"

"Sorry. U were on my mind."
"U2."
"So, u wanna do something?"
Well, right now I gotta do hw, but yes, I wud."
"Cool!"
"Got a questions 4u"
"Ya?"
"Does ur dad hire out to individuals??
"Um, I think so. Why?"
"Cuz... mom wants to hire a detective & I thot of ur dad."
"Waz up?"
"Long story. Can I tell u n person?"
"Ya."
"So... can u ask ur dad?"
"Yup. He's not home right now, but as soon as he gets here."

"K. Thanks." I sighed and resigned myself to doing dreaded homework. Spanish.

It wasn't so bad. It was just a lot of memorization. *Then* it was application, but I had to do a whole lot of memorization before the application part. My brain was just not committed this afternoon. I did force it to cooperate, though. I started with index cards. Half way through memorization, Jacob texted me back.

"Dad said we cud meet & discuss details 2night. What ya doing at 7?
"I'll ask mom. That shud b fine."
I found Mom and told her the news.
"Where are we meeting?" she asked me.
"I'm not sure, Mom. I'll find out."

We decided to meet Big Whiskey's in Nixa. It was a local restaurant on one side, bar on the other. We could eat a bite, sit outside where the conversation would be a little more private, and discuss terms and conditions.

Mom and I got ready. It almost felt like a double date. Mom wore jeans and a nice summer shirt; it was dressy but not overly so. It definitely showed her more feminine side. I wore shorts and a summer blouse. We both touched up our hair and makeup.

We showed up about fifteen minutes early and secured a table. Within five minutes of us sitting down, we heard the loud rumble of Harleys. It was the men we were waiting on!

Jacob's Harley was a Dyno Series Street Glide with a really cool paint job done in greens, purple, and silver accented by thicker black fingers of paint dripping and crossing randomly. His father had a Fatboy with the works. The chrome extras, many of which contained flaming skulls, complemented the black background with maroon ghost flames etched in the paint. Both Mom and I got up to admire the popular motorcycles.

Fifteen minutes later, we were seated, and everyone had ordered hamburgers and fries. We made our introductions, and I sensed a growing vibe of interest between Mom and Jacob's dad, Jason. We received our drinks before the conversation really got down to business.

"So I'm told that our meeting was more of a business endeavor?" Jason began.

"Yes," Mom said. "I don't know what the kids have told you…"

Jacob's brows shot up, and he sent me an inquisitive look.

"I, ah, haven't really… mentioned what was going on…" I said uneasily and shifted in my seat.

"Okay. Laurie doesn't like to be the center of attention," Mom began, "But I'm tired of this. TIRED!" Mom slammed her fist on the table, startling us all.

When she saw our looks of surprise, she said, "I'm so sorry. I'm just not handling this well at all."

Mom appeared choked with emotions, so I butted in, "I am being stalked by the murderer of that girl. The one who looks similar to me," I revealed. Both men's heads swiveled to stare at me, open-mouthed. "Um, Jacob, don't be upset with me. I've really only talked with you one-to-one last night at the party. It's not something that I could just randomly bring up…"

He gently said, "Well, it *was* brought up. You could have mentioned it without it being random."

"I know, but I'd just met you. I didn't want you to think me a drama queen."

His eyes swirled olive with emotions. I could tell he cared. "I guess I can understand," he admitted after a pause.

"Tell me *exactly* what's been going on," Jason instructed. We filled him in on every detail concerning "Adam".

"Yes, of course I'll take the job!" Jason said vehemently.

"Oh, great!" Mom said with relief. "What do you think you'll charge?"

"Not much. I'd almost do it for free!"

"Oh, I couldn't ask you to do that!"

"Believe me, I want to. My son cares about your daughter. And, uh, I wouldn't mind… seeing if you'd like to, um, go out… sometime… with me?"

Mom looked pleased yet uncomfortable at the same time. "I'd like to," she said with a pause, "but do you think it's wise? To mix business and dating, I mean?"

"Well, if I take it upon my own shoulders to do this job, it wouldn't be business, now, would it?"

"Dad's been following this case very closely," Jacob revealed. "He hates people who abuse women and children."

I saw Mom's eyes soften a bit. I knew it was brownie points in her book.

"I was pretty much informally investigating the case from a distant point of view," Jason said. "But now I have a vested interest! I won't let some maniac take out or cause two beautiful women panic or fear!"

"I'd be happy to pay you!" Mom said.

"I won't hear of it. I'm sure there'll be some sort of police reward if I can apprehend this guy," Jason said.

"Won't that be dangerous?" Mom asked.

"Nah. I'm good at being precautious."

"It still doesn't feel right for me to offer to hire you to do a job then you decide to do it for free."

"I was doing it for free anyway. It was just a tad more informal than it'll be now."

Jacob was nodding his head in agreement.

"So that's why you seemed really knowledgeable about the goings-on during the murder conversation last night," I said.

Again, Jacob nodded.

"Well," Mom sounded unsure, "only if you're certain?"

Jason nodded. "And if you'd rather wait until after this guy is apprehended to see me, I can be patient. Good things come to those who wait," he said with a wink. Then he paused a second for effect before adding, "but I'd really like to see you."

"I'd like that, too," Mom whispered. "I wouldn't mind seeing you now, but I'll warn you that I'm preoccupied by my daughter's safety until this guy is off the streets!"

"No one can blame you there," Jason consoled. "But it's a deal!" He made Mom shake on it.

When the men saw us looking once more toward theirbikes, they promised to bring extra helmets on some night and take us for a ride. Both of us thought that sounded like fun.

We watched the guys ready themselves to ride then kick their bikes to life. It certainly wasn't a necessity, but we felt complimented when they followed us to see us safely home.

Once we walked in the quiet house, we threw our things down on the table. Half the time, the table was used more for a collection of things rather than a place to eat.

"See, Mom? You teased me about Jacob. I guess it's time for fair play." I instigated.

"Yes, baby, you sure do know how to pick them! Jason is *handsome!* And tall!"

"I know! I think he's probably a little over an inch taller than Jacob! I think he's at least 6'7"!"

Mom nodded with dreamy eyes as she pulled out her laptop to begin some work.

"I guess I'll head upstairs to work on some more homework."

"Okay, baby. We can watch a movie later, if you want." "K. That would be nice."

I headed up the darkened staircase to work on my Spanish. I put my hand on the smooth, cool wood of the beautiful banister and suddenly, a chill electrified its way up my arm. My breath quickened in my throat, and my heart began to pound.

I abruptly turned around and headed back down the stairs. I feigned missing something to help me with my work. Spooky music was playing in my head, but I refused to be the proverbial girl that walks down the dark hallway to her death with the audience yelling out, "Don't go in there!"I silently crept back in the kitchen where Mom was sitting and whispered calmly in her ear. Her eyes became silver dollars, but she quietly slipped the laptop under her arm, grabbed her purse, and we headed back out the door.

I texted Jacob right when we reached the safety of the car. Immediately, he responded. *"I'll be right over. Get the heck outta there!"*

"We're leaving now. I think u shud wait 4 the police". "But dad & I have many of the same rights that police do – only we don't hafta b quite so… political."

"Still, Jacob. Who knows if he has a gun? Idk if he's even n there 4 sure. I wasn't gonna look!"

"Good. But something made u think he was."

Mom backed the car up, and we zoomed away. Within minutes, we were at the police station.

"Here we are again," I mumbled. "By the way, mom, we need the cops to check our house out there ASAP. Jason and Jacob are probably there now."

"Why do you say that?"

"Because I… sort of… texted Jacob."

"Oh."

We filled out the paperwork and an officer was dispersed to the location. We drove back as well. We couldn't stand the not-knowing-what-was-going-on feeling. When we pulled up, the police lights were flashing blue, red, and white while Jason and Jacob were waiting for us on the front lawn.

Almost before I could open the door, Jacob said, "Laurie, you *do* seem to know things! It was obvious that pedophile was in your room, but he managed to get out right before Dad and I pulled up!"

"How could you tell!?" Mom blurted out.

Jason came up behind mom and placed a calming hand on her elbow. "We saw where he'd jimmied her window and where he'd hidden himself in her closet."

Mom's hand flew over her mouth, and her eyes welled up with tears. She allowed Jason's arm to circle her and draw her in closer to his body, and she appeared to draw strength from his support.

Jacob stood by me to console, but I didn't know how I felt yet. The shock of the moment had passed me by. I'm sure it would return to strike out at me, but for the moment, I was handling everything calmly.

We saw the policeman approaching. "It appears to be clear, ma'am," he said gently to my mother. "We've really nothing to go on, but I can do some drive bys to help keep an eye on the situation."

"Thank you, Officer," Mom managed to say. He shook our hands before returning to his car.

Jason looked down into Mom's face, "Look, KaLissa, I know you don't really know me because we just met and all, but would you consider staying at my house? We have a large guest room –."

"I don't know, Jason. I really appreciate it. Let me think about it."

"Fair enough."

We all walked in the house and took a seat in the living room.

"Mom. I think I'd like to stay at Jacob's house, if you don't mind," I blurted out. "I just feel so… unsafe right now. If we stayed there, at least Jason knows how to apprehend people and can use guns."

"Okay, baby. I just don't want your reputation to suffer."

"It won't. I just don't want to die in order to save my reputation. If people really know me, they'll trust my honor. If they want to start silly rumors, let them. I don't care about what those kinds of people think anyway."

"I know. Okay, we will. But if those rumors start, you let me know. Rumors can damage more than you think."

Chapter Five

Mom and I gathered the things we'd need and locked up the house. Then we got in our car and followed the Toyota Tundra over to Jason's residence. They lived on a quiet piece of land with a comfortable house. It was two stories with four bedrooms and a garage. A large male Akita decorated their lawn.

We got out of the cars tentatively, warily watching the beautiful canine.

"Tank won't hurt you. He knows you're friends of ours," Jacob reassured.

"However, he's a great deterrent to guys like the one who broke into your house," Jason added. "He'll protect you with every ounce in him."

Tank, a powerfully built silver pinto with a black overlay and mask, came up to sniff hello. He wagged his handsomely curled tail to show us he accepted us. Then he rooted his large black nose under my hand for me to pet him. I scratched behind his triangular ears and watched his brown eyes halfway close in ecstasy.

"He's really just a big baby," Jason admitted. Halfheartedly, I left the big dog to take my possessions into our temporary room.

The interior of the house was very rustic, made solely from split logs, many of which retained the bark, and smoothed to a fine sheen. The banisters and stairs were all hand crafted by Jacob's father and grandfather. We followed the men up the circular staircase that opened into a half floor that overlooked the living room.

A full bath and a spacious guest room were just off the small second sitting room. The bedroom given to us to use was painted in soft blues with one wall a darker hue. A large oil painting of a beautiful castle surrounded by flower gardens adorned the darker wall. A 48" flat screen television was anchored to one corner in the room, and a queen four-poster was made up with a brilliantly crafted homemade quilt.

An antique vanity occupied one section of the wall and was separated by a few feet from a large oak desk. On the other side, a dresser, chest of drawers, and a curio cabinet happily gave compliments to each other. This room would be perfect, I decided.

"Now I can give you two different rooms if you insist," Jason began, "but for safety purposes, sharing this room or if one of you would sleep on the couch in the small sitting room right there would be ideal," he paused to point, "The couch is comfortable as is, or I can make it into a bed. If you two are very close in proximity, you can be more aware of any unusual noises. I really don't think that jerk will try to break in here with Tank on the prowl, though."

"Mom, sharing a bed is fine," I said. "I'm tired of being scared. I think I might feel better if we're in the same room. You just have to promise not to steal all the covers!"

"Wait a minute. You're the one to steal the covers!" Mom denied. She turned to look up at Jason and answered, "Yes, we'll just share the guest room."

The guys bowed out gracefully to give us the space we needed. It was sort of uncomfortable "moving in" with two guys who were, in essence, complete strangers. Nevertheless, I felt I was a pretty good judge of character, and I had a good vibe about this decision. Besides, they both were *very* handsome. I hid a smile.

Both Mom and I slept well but light our first night. It was nice to feel safe, but just the fact that it wasn't *home* made a regular night's sleep light. Although we were in someone else's house, things seemed fairly normal.

Right away I texted my friends to tell them the latest news. They were irate at the turn of events, but they agreed that we were safer in the presence of two men who knew how to handle hoodlums. Murders, however, might be a different story.

School went well that week. It was nice waking up and sharing breakfast together with Jason and Jacob. We quickly were becoming very good friends. My other friends welcomed Jacob with loving arms into our little "clique".

Thursday morning promised to be a hot one. I asked Mom if Jacob could give me a ride to school on his Harley. She agreed if he promised to not drive excessively fast or dangerously.

I was excited and nervous when I placed a few of my school things in his black studded saddle bags. I secured my hair in a braid and placed the black Harley helmet on my head.

"You sure you want to do this?" Jacob asked.

I nodded. I was sure my eyes were large, but I anticipated the feel of the breeze cooling my skin. Jacob started his bike with a dimpled grin, and I climbed on behind his large frame.

"I don't have a sissy bar, yet," Jacob said, "so you'll just have to hang onto my waist."

I smiled and said, "Are you calling me a sissy?" He answered with a deep chuckle that I could only read into as foreshadowing, but I wrapped my arms as far as they would go around him anyway, and we zoomed off. The acceleration was invigorating! I felt the wind play and tug at my braid, and the airstream caressed my body. It was even better than I imagined! Before I knew it, we were at school. All our buddies came up to *ooh* and *ahh* at the super cool Harley.

"Now I feel famous," I joked with a wink.

"You ride like a pro," Jacob complimented. "Are you sure you haven't ridden before?"

I shook my head, and all my friends laughed and walked into the building with us. I was on a personal high all day at school, and I looked forward to sitting behind the attractive Harley rider on the way home.

After school, my friends and I jogged. In my opinion, the day couldn't get much better. Jason had texted me to say that he and his father wanted to take Mom and me out to eat for supper.

"Where?" I asked him as I readied myself to ride.

"I'm not sure, but I think Dad mentioned the Texas Roadhouse."

"Oh, awesome! I LOVE that place!" I said with relish. "Yes,
    it's pretty hard to beat a steak if you ask me,"
Jacob agreed.

He hopped on and started his Harley, and I climbed on the back of the vibrating machine. The familiar rush of sensation fluttered my stomach. As we accelerated on the highway, Jacob reached one arm down and patted my thigh. I smiled even though I knew he couldn't see it.

We had been traveling about ten minutes toward Jacob's house when, unexpectedly, a frigid wintery gust blasted at my body. Invisible icy fingers grabbed and tore at my clothing, and I was immediately fearful that I'd fall off. Jacob didn't appear to notice the drastic change in the temperature. However, I clutched at his body frantically with frozen fingers.

"What's wrong?" he asked back over his shoulder. "Don't you *feel that*?" I shouted through chattering teeth.

"Feel what?" he asked.

"Jacob, please pull over. I feel strange… in a bad way."

"We've only got three miles to go until we're at the house. Do you still want me to pull over?"

"Please?"

Jacob reluctantly did as requested. He pulled the Harley onto a gravel side road that led back into some woods.

"Go back toward the tree line," I whispered urgently.

"What?"

"Do it, Jacob! *Do it now!*"

Without more debate, Jacob keyed up the idle, and we swept back toward the woods. He shut the bike off and turned toward me.

"Now what's this all about?" he asked softly. His eyes filled with worry when he saw my ashen complexion and my uncontrollable chattering of my teeth. "Laurie! What's wrong? Are you going to be sick?"

"Put your arms around me. I'm so cold."

Jacob gently lifted me from the bike and cradled me in his arms. I felt as if I was experiencing what someone dying surely had to feel. It was as if all my strength and warmth had been zapped from me. My limbs were stiff and rigid, similar I imagined, to what *rigor mortis* does as the soul leaves the case of the body behind.

Jacob sat on the ground, pulled me in, and wrapped me up with his strong arms. My head rested against his chiseled chest. His large hands vigorously rubbed up and down my arms to restore some heat. We sat like that for ten minutes.

Then, as quickly as the coldness had hit, the heat returned. With it came knowledge; I'd saved our lives in that moment.

"Jacob! Look!" I pointed toward the highway.

Slowly driving down the road from the direction of Jacob's house was the blacked out Charger.

"It's *him*!" I revealed.

Jacob stood up and gently placed me on the ground.

"Jacob! What are you doing?"

"I'm going to follow this jerk!" "You can't do that! He'll kill us."

"You're not going. You're going to stay here and call the police and our parents."

"No! You don't have any way to protect yourself!"

"I'm not going to be stupid, Laurie. I'll be careful. I'm not going to let him see me."

"You're not exactly inconspicuous on a Harley, Jacob." He ignored me and hopped on his bike.

"Jacob! Don't go!!! Please! *Please!*" I begged.

"Laurie, I have to. Call it a man thing. No one is going to get away with this!"

And with that, he zoomed off toward the street.

I called the police and our parents. They could hear the panic in my voice. I did my best to describe my location.

Suddenly, the roar of a Harley barreling back down the highway with the scream of car rubber hot on his heels made me drop my phone. All I could do was watch as I saw the devil disguised as a Dodge try to ram the figure on the bike. Without realizing it, a scream ripped from my throat. I began running toward the action.

It was then that I realized what I'd done. How the car driver saw me, I'll never know. Apparently, the Harley was no longer of interest. The car did a perfect forty-five degree right turn toward me when he was perpendicular to the gravel road. All I could see was the storm of dust boiling from the car as he gunned it toward me.

My body took over and I ran as hard as I could back to the tree line. I had no idea if I'd make it or not. Thank God I'd taken Jacob's advice. Surely the police were on the way!

I hit the tree line simultaneously as the car slid to a stop. I heard the car door open and instantly, footsteps were racing toward me. I felt my backbone stiffen and goose bumps raced up and down my spine. My legs developed a mind of their own. They suddenly ran faster without me meaning for them to.

Then I heard the most welcomed sound in my life: A Harley. Jacob roared down the tree line. I angled my direction back toward him. Consequently, so did "Adam". He was going to try to intercept me! Jacob and I would have a fighting chance with two to one odds as long as Adam didn't have a knife or a gun. Still, I had no desire to find out!

I was naturally a runner, but that didn't mean I sprinted. In spite of that, I gave it my all. I jumped toward Jacob just as his muscular arm caught me and swung me up behind him. At that precise moment, Adam made a spectacular dive at us and only missed us by about three feet. I couldn't help myself; I screamed and clutched Jacob hysterically.

We raced back toward Jacob's home where safety awaited us. There we'd find weapons to even the playing field. By the time we'd reached the highway, Adam had reached his car.

"Are you sure we shouldn't go back to town – toward the police station?" I managed to yell above the roar of the engine.

"We'll never make it. He's got a hot rod in that car. We'll be lucky to make it home in one piece. Hang on, baby!"

Within moments, the black dragon was breathing on our heels. Jacob raced like a madman to stay just out of reach of the monster's chomping fangs, but only by inches. I was glad he knew how to take the turns expertly. It was frightening how the bike nearly lay on the asphalt as it sliced around the turns. Finally, the house was within sight.

"Here's where he has a chance," Jacob warned. The place where the asphalt turned and his drive began was white chat. It would be difficult to maneuver without crashing the bike at this speed. I tucked my head against Jacob's back and prayed.

Just when I thought we were going to make it, the demon reached out a claw and bumped the tire. Jacob managed to stabilize and slow our speed to a degree, but he'd lost control of the machine. The Charger saw the moment of weakness and attacked again, this time with more punch. We couldn't endure the hit and remain upright.

Jacob clutched at me, but the speed and velocity made his attempts useless. We both tumbled in different directions. The car stopped a second time, but on this occasion, it wasn't the same careless fashion.

Both Jacob and I remained in the position our bodies assumed once we stopped rolling from the crash, unable to move. I didn't know how badly I was injured, but I was positive some bones were broken. At least I wasn't dead… yet. I hoped Jacob fared as well. I couldn't crane my head to look and see where he was or what was going on.

An evil laugh filled the air. "You, my spry little monkey, are a hard one to catch. No matter. I enjoyed the thrill of the chase. I'm nearly disappointed that this is almost over." The statement was followed by harsher, throaty laughter.

"Jacob…" I heard my gravelly voice rasp.

"Oh, he's alive, my pretty. I care not if he lives or dies. You're another matter entirely." He stooped down over me and laughed for a third time. It was a deep laugh that caused him to arch his head back. I cracked a swollen eye open. The sun glittered down on the edge of a sharp knife grasped firmly in his hand. My eyes widened. I assumed I'd be gutted like a deer where I lay.

"No, my dear, not here," he answered as if reading my mind. "You'll be rewarded for such an intriguing game you played of evading me! I've a plan for you, Beautiful, but it involves more time and energy than I spent with your twin. You'll live until I tire of your company. I see from your position that I won't have much difficulty with you fighting against me." A hint of a smile touched his hard mouth.

I felt my body being lifted again. I tried to struggle against his superior strength, but my unwilling body was drained. I had no energy left to fight. I shrieked as the pain coursed through my body.

Adam turned and hoisted me over his back like a sack of potatoes. I screamed as pain carved patterns through my ribs. A sharp stabbing sensation stole my breath away. Adam, conscious of the degree of my pain, decided to carry me in his arms.

"I want you awake for the first stages of our time together," he informed me.

Out of nowhere, Jacob materialized and blocked Adam's path back to his car. Adam smiled sardonically at Jacob. "You think you can stop me? You may be bigger than me, young man, but you're injured. I, however, am not."

Jacob's breathing was labored, but I knew he would give his last breath for me. In fact, that may be just what he was doing.

"Still don't want to move out of my way?" mocked Adam. "Well, I can slice your girlfriend up right now while you watch, or I can string your organs all over this farm!" For effect, Adam clutched me with one arm and sliced his blade through the air with his other. I wheezed and coughed in agony as the pressure of his arm ripped throbbing sensations throughout my body. Still, Jacob would not move.

Adam slid me to the ground to give Jacob his full attention. He knew from my condition that there was no escape for me. All I could do was watch helplessly and whimper.

Adam approached Jacob. He was nimble and quick on his feet. Jacob, on the other hand, moved stiffly and his breathing was labored and quick. I imagined he also had bruised or broken ribs.

Adam lunged at Jacob and managed to lay a strip of meat open on his arm.

"NO!" I managed to scream airily.

Jacob wheezed out a breath of pain, but still maintained his position.

Adam moved in again and slashed and sliced at Jacob. Finally, Jacob managed to counter with a lightning fast lunge and grabbed a hold of Adam's arm which sent the knife flying. Adam, nevertheless, was not discouraged. He laughed disdainfully and countered the move with ease. He feigned a punch to Jacob's face and then kicked his feet out from under him. Jacob landed with a groan.

Adam was immediately on him, pummeling away at him.

Jacob did not move after a few swift kicks. Adam stopped to say, "Now I'm going to kill you for that. And your little girlfriend is going to watch."

Slowly and dramatically, Adam retrieved his knife. Then

he turned and walked back to Jacob, exaggerating his steps. Blood was already pooling under Jacob's cut arm.

"You'd better go," I croaked. "I called the police. They'll be here any time!"

"Don't worry, my pretty girl. We'll leave. I just need to slice a few spots here and there on this… *boy*. Then we'll go."

He moved toward Jacob and stooped over his fallen body. His blade was getting closer to the athlete. Adam ripped open Jacob's shirt and decided where he'd begin his first slice.

"*No, No NO! NO!!!*" I managed to screech.

Adam dramatized his intentions by swinging his knife high in the air until I could only focus on the rust-colored blade. Then he began a downward forceful motion. Unexpectedly, a silver and white streak of fur pounced on the man like Harry Potter capturing the golden snitch. Tank clamped his mouth down on Adam's forearm and wouldn't release it. A ferocious growl erupted from deep within his throat.

"Good boy," I croaked.

The dog rolled the man onto his back and stood over him, snarling viciously. He was inches above Adam's throat. I think Adam understood what would happen to him if he dared to defy the powerful animal.

Cars began pulling up. Mom and Jason sped to where we were. They were followed seconds later by the police.

"Oh, my God, baby!" Mom crooned over me.

"Check Jacob," I rasped. "Is he… Okay?"

"He's alive," Jason yelled to us. He was trying to stop his wound from bleeding.

Mom called an ambulance.

Because I knew we were safe, a soft black blanket took

away my pain and perception. The next thing I was aware of was waking up in the hospital. Jacob and I were sharing a room, beginning the process of recovery.

I had a broken clavicle and a few broken ribs. Bruises covered me from head to toe, and my eyes were blacked and swollen. Luckily, my nose only had a hairline fracture.

Jacob also suffered broken ribs and several fractures. His arm was stitched back. He'd had to receive a transfusion due to his blood loss, but he'd also make a full recovery.

Jason and Mom stayed by our sides. My friends came to visit every chance they could. I thanked God repeatedly for his support; I felt we'd have been dead without His protection.

"Mom, what happened to… to… Adam?"

"He's in jail, honey. He'll have to wait right there until his trial. He's going to be put away for a very long time."

"Will we have to testify?"

"I'm sure you will, honey, unless they can find that girl's body. But we don't have to think about that for a while."

A pretty young nurse entered the room and suddenly I felt like all the heat had been sucked out of the room;

Suddenly, the frigid temperatures of Antarctica filled the area. Goosebumps erupted on my body. The dark-haired beauty smiled vacantly and said, "The doctor will be here shortly to make sure you're all ready to go!"

"Thanks, dear," Mom responded.

Perhaps Mom didn't notice how the black pits in the nurse's eyes were bottomless, a vacant pool devoid of emotion. The young woman's beauty did detract from her behavior that, in my opinion, had to cover a realm of sociopathic tendencies. She turned to face me while she patted my leg. I struggled to breathe when I saw her eyes *had no soul.*

Fiercely, I clutched at Mom and pulled her to me in a desperate hug.

"Honey, what's a matter?" she asked.

"I–I'll tell you… in a minute," I managed.

Mom held my hand when I finally released her. I was happy for the warmth of her love. It helped to offset the arctic blast from the nurse. I warily watched her do chores before leaving the room. Silence followed in her wake for a few long moments.

"Does it have something to do with that nurse, Honey?" Mom asked me gently.

"Yes! Mom, her eyes have no soul!" I cried.

Both Jacob and Jason were looking at me in concerned consideration.

"Please," I said, "have her checked out!"

"I'll see what I can do, sweetie, but…" her voice trailed off.

"Looks like we may have another job to investigate when you're recovered, Son," Jason said.

Jacob nodded. Then he winked at me and said, "We'll get right on that!"

Sheri Chapman

More from Sheri Chapman:

My website: https://prayerpawpuppies.wixsite.com/authorsherichapman/books

Books

Wild Passion *(Book 1 of the Passion series – historical romance)*

Wild Dreams Publishing

Wild Passion is COMING TO THE MOVIE SCREEN!!!

(It will be PG13 and renamed "Captive Heart")

*filming begins in 2019

BOOKS coming in 2019:

Passions of the Heart *(Book 2 of the Passion series – coming soon in 2019)*

Wild Dreams Publishing

Werewolves Don't Like Green Beans - *(Book 1 of Wolves Unchained) Wild Dreams Publishing*

Protectors of the People - *(Book 2 of Wolves Unchained) Wild Dreams Publishing*

Anthologies 2018

For Melissa: An Anthology: **"My Shadow"** *– Wild Dreams Publishing*

Rags to Riches: Cinderella Love Stories (Anthology): **"Recovering the Magic"** –

A Wild Dreams Christmas: From Our House to Yours (Anthology): **"A Humble Christmas"** –   *Hydra Productions*

Wild Dreams Publishing

Christmas Fairytales 2018 (Anthology): **"Shooting for Christmas"** – Hydra Productions

<u>Anthologies coming in 2019</u>
Romantic Interludes: Paranormal Romance: **"A Little Bermuda Love"** – Stained Glass Publishing

Reincarnation Anthology: **"A Killer, Revisited"** – *Wild Dreams Publishing*

Chasing Your Wildest Dreams – **"Chief Spirit Bear: Rise to Power** – A Passion series story" – *Wild Dreams Publishing*

Just a Drop: Vampire Anthology: (Untitled at this point) – *Wild Dreams Publishing*

Calendar Themed Anthologies (Volume 1 Fantasy/Paranormal): (Untitled at this point) – *Wild Dreams Publishing*

Calendar Themed Anthologies (Volume 3 Horror): **"Predatory Evil"** – *Wild Dreams Publishing*

To stay up to date with Sheri Chapman, you can follow her at any, or all, of these sites:

Facebook Account (personal): https://www.facebook.com/sheri.branson.3

Facebook Page (author): https://www.facebook.com/AuthorSheriChapman/

Goodreads: https://www.goodreads.com/author/show/8332075.Sheri_Chapman

Wattpad: http://wattpad.com/user/SheriChapman

Linked-In: https://www.linkedin.com/in/sheri-chapman-a256276a/

Twitter: https://twitter.com/Sheri7303